DARBYSHIRE
WELCOME TO THE JUNGLE

Maverick Alexander

Illustrated by Rodrigo Merched

Maverick Alexander

Enjoy.

First Edition

 @darbyshireusa

info@darbyshireusa.com

Dedication

This one is for my best friends, without whom I wouldn't have had the inspiration to take what I do for fun and turn it into something greater.

I also wish to thank my parents, who have never stopped believing in me, through thick and thin.

Finally, I extend a massive and special thanks to Rodrigo, the incredibly talented illustrator who took a chance by walking around inside my imagination with me. Thank you for your help in bringing these characters to life!

Table of Contents

Darbyshire: Welcome to the Jungle
Copyright © 2018 Gwabboh LLC

Preface:
WELCOME TO DARBYSHIRE!

Greetings from Darbyshire, a town where some wacky and offensive characters live and interact. This is the first book of the series, and introduces a handful of characters in stories where they have limited contact with one another, although they all live in the fictitious city of Darbyshire.

We follow this motley crew through a wide range of experiences, as the stories are told in a politically incorrect, fantastical fashion. These stories are fictional, satirical, purposefully hyperbolic, and not meant to be taken too seriously.

What can silly stories about animals tell us about human nature?

What do the stories tell you about yourself?

Strong men create good times,
Good times create weak men,
Weak men create hard times,
Hard times create strong men.

I just lost the game.

BRETT THE CAT

Brett Whiskers is the most sophisticated cat to ever exist, unequivocally. He's 6'4, 230 pounds, and jacked. He wears a tuxedo whenever possible. Although he stands upright and tall like a human, in all seriousness, he's a cat. His thick fur looks as though God took a personal day and said, "World hunger? Seems a bit pedestrian. I'm going to put all my effort into making a really good-looking cat today."

The only thing more robust than Brett's investment portfolio and sexual market value is his ability to turn down the sexual advances of narcissistically egocentric, godless women. Of course, it isn't necessarily all their faults, as modern hookup culture, higher education, and female empowerment coupled with psychologically manipulative media and advertising subtly encourages them to be selfish divorce pirates whose future parenting skills would expedite the collapse of western civilization. Brett has no time for such folly. His policy is that if a gal has any social media accounts, she probably isn't wife material. Not a bad rule.

Brett Whiskers is an entrepreneur and a philanthropist. When he's not busy crushing the stock market, building his real estate empire, and making businesses flush with cash, he's volunteering and passing out participation certificates at schools for the mentally retarded—Arizona State and the University of Arizona. He gets it.

The secret to Brett's success is that he's a shameless patriot. Brett makes Uncle Sam look like a subversive Marxist flag burner by comparison. Brett drives a Ford F-150, lifted, with 96% tinted windows. Brett smokes Marlboro Reds and never turns down a high-five. When asked by the Democratic Party chairman to donate, Brett threw him out of his private plane without a parachute. Whisky, AKA Brett Whiskers, loves the New England Patriots, and every year at Tom Brady's birthday, Tom introduces Brett as "the key behind his success." Bill Belichick often remarks postgame that Brett hiked him the playbook that he kicked through the field goal of life.

Brett's origin story truly started in college in the mid-2000s. He was accepted to every Ivy League school on full rides, either for academics or athletics. Every school wanted him to attend to add bottomless prestige to their institutions. Didn't matter. Brett couldn't have cared less. He decided to attend Darbyshire University. He showed up on campus, and the co-eds could sense his overflowing levels of testosterone. The floors of the dormitories were consistently marked with "caution, wet floor" janitorial signs, for quietly obvious reasons.

During introduction week, the entire student body began to hear whispers of the new cat in town, Brett Whiskers. He was a complete enigma. Everyone wanted to be friends with the jacked anthropomorphic cat. Every athletic team in the school wanted to name him team captain, even if they didn't know if Brett played the sport. The fraternities changed the name of "rush week" to "Brett Week." The alumni association filed a formal petition to get the school mascot changed from the Grizzlies to the "Brett."

Brett double majored in Business Administration and Pleasure Studies. His professors could tell he possessed the multidisciplinary genius to truly understand the relationship between business and pleasure.

Brett's academic success was mirrored perfectly by his social aptitude. He was the life of every party he attended for a few reasons: he had an arsenal of dance moves that made Michael Jackson look like he may have suffered from muscular dystrophy, he could put down 20 beers in a single sitting without showing any signs of impairment, and he could induce a female orgasm with a hard wink. He knew with great power came great responsibility, so he routinely advised blacked-out sorority girls to call their dads.

The only thing more incredible than Brett's ability to make the teachers and administrators at Darbyshire University quit, by way of capitalistic intellectual checkmate, was his ability to give electrifying speeches. B-Dub would routinely stop classes and parties alike to riff on the finer points of civic duty, the importance of fiscal responsibility, and why feminism is a joke. Brett was a trendsetter who boldly wore jean shorts, American flag cutoffs, and aviators.

Fast-forward to present-day. Brett Whiskers sits in his high-rise apartment, practicing his Chinese in the mirror. "Wǒ tǎoyàn kǒngbù fèn zi!" he yells, with the intonation and eloquence of a native speaker. Brett walks from his bathroom to his walk-in closet. First he outfits himself with a Kevlar vest, then one of his signature tuxedos. "Today is possibly the biggest day of my life," he remarks to himself as he looks in the mirror. He then proceeds to his secret armory where he equips himself with an RPG and heat seeking rockets. B-Dub is on a mission: A mission to change the future by altering the past.

Brett Whiskers steps into his personal time machine and sets the date for September 11th, 2001. In a flash of lightning-charged, turbo-powered mayhem, B-Dub finds himself standing next to the World Trade Center. He sees a plane heading for tower one. "We built this city on rock and roll, mother fucker," Brett exclaims as he launches a heat-seeking rocket towards the plane. The plane explodes, and Brett high-fives a group of Chinese tourists. "Wǒ tǎoyàn kǒngbù fèn zi, folks, nothing to see here!" B-dub shouts, knowing that practicing Chinese was the right thing to do. The second plane approaches, but Brett is ready. Brett whispers under his breath, "Hi, my name is Brett, and I'd like to tell you about our lord and savior Jesus Christ," as he fires off another heat-seeking rocket at plane number 2. The plane explodes and crashes into the street, completely annihilating a Manhattan traffic jam.

Women flock to B-Dub and assault him with a barrage of soaked panties and unbuckled bras. Brett thankfully brought a sharpie to sign all of the busty women's chests. The women with small to medium sized breasts are disappointed, but Brett smiles at them and remarks, "Ladies, I'm Brett Whiskers, and at the end of the day, I'm an ass man." Women start fainting.

Brett then takes out his cell phone and speed dials NORAD. He informs them that there's a plane heading for the pentagon, and they should torch it. "Who is this and how did you get this phone number?" the operator asks. "I'm Brett H. Whiskers, and I just prevented 9-11."

The End.

BANANA FINGERS

Our protagonist sits at his desk in his office. He punches in numbers and calculations into his macro-laden Excel interface. He's a bottom-line oriented businessman who knows the value of synergistic marketing, and people-first sales. His name is Banana Fingers, and he's a silverback gorilla turned gym owner. B. Fingers is a work-hard, play-hard kind of boss. What he lacks in pleasantry, he makes up for in 800-pound bench press. When he greets new clients, his enormous hands silently communicate: "You're in my house now, there's no turning back, and with a little work, you can possess the strength to not feel like an effeminate pussy when you greet me."

Dr. Banana Fingers got his Ph.D. in Kinesiology from the National Institute of Endangered Species Who Lift. He failed to take any ethics courses or gender sensitivity courses, because they sounded about as useful as reading a pamphlet on self-castration.

Today is employee appreciation day, and B. Fingers has pulled out all the stops. The staff room has been transformed into a veritable dining hall fit for a king. He bought all the fine trimmings: Gatorade, pizza, and napkins. Dr. Fingers wants to throw a party showing his appreciation for the current staff members, especially after all the heat he's been taking over the past few months from multiple employees suing him over sexual harassment claims.

That's a risk a male business owner takes with a predominantly or even partially female staff at a gym, or most places for that matter. Hell hath no fury like a woman scorned, and as a male working closely with women who understand the social and legal advantages and protections afforded to them, Banana Fingers had to be wary of lawsuits and swift paths to professional implosion. #NotAllWomen

Losing one's livelihood and community reputation was commonplace these days, as an accusation of misconduct was sufficient to obliterate a man without due process. In many workplaces where women do not have a dress code other than to cover the nipples and nether regions, nor any reason *not* to use their sexual leverage for personal gain, modern business was a gamble. The judicial system made this an absolute certainty.

Although he was well aware of the business and personal liability he had to endure as a result of having women as colleagues, Banana Fingers had an impossibly difficult time staying the course and maintaining entirely professional and platonic relationships with the most attractive staff members. B. Fingers was, after all, a high testosterone stud, and rewiring his brain and endocrine system based on the laws of modern society was impossible.

Banana Fingers was lucky enough to have earned his Chad Privilege, though. He worked out consistently, ate well, read books, and had his own business. Attractive females tend to allow alpha males like Banana Fingers quite a bit more leeway than they would if Banana Fingers were a low-T pushover like 87.333% of the men in the world. Banana Fingers didn't have to rely on virtue signaling, dishonesty, or feminist appeasement to gain favor with women, and could get away with fairly brazen sexual hoodwinks with his foxy trainers, as they all found him bold, handsome, and playful. He also had a huge pipe, which the ladies didn't hate, either.

A few months ago, B. Fingers had installed cameras in the female locker room, insisting to the staff it was a safety issue. Nobody believed him, but didn't make a big deal out of it, because the trainers were all vying for his affection, as well as pay raises, and didn't want to spoil their shot at getting either. Banana Fingers became emboldened because the camera operation went so smoothly. He then installed a glory hole between his office and the female showers. He explained it was part of a new ventilation system to keep the showers smelling fresh. It was a sloppy explanation at best, but Chad Privilege saved the day, and nobody complained.

When two of his trainers asked him point-blank to have a threesome in exchange for a pay raise, Dr. Fingers understandably couldn't resist. The female trainers' gambit to utilize their sexuality for money was successful, but it didn't result in a lawsuit, as the trainers fully understood the offer they themselves had proposed, and had gotten everything they intended to. Stacy Privilege was a thing, too.

Where B. Fingers went wrong was with his daycare staff. The two women in charge were sexually frustrated feminazis, who didn't recognize Banana Fingers' Chad Privilege, as he was WAY out of their league. Big B. Fingers was far too focused on hiring competent, positive, healthy, and attractive female trainers, and forgot that depressed, out-of-shape women who wanted to change the workplace in their image might not be beneficial to his business model that revolved entirely around being healthy and happy.

Within a week of being hired, both Amy and Randi, the sexually repulsive fat women who were 3's who fancied themselves 8's, had already accused B. Fingers of crossing the line for a handful of alleged offenses: He didn't greet them with their proper pronouns of Zer and Bork. He walked by them with "patriarchy" in his eyes. He "mansplained" the duties of the job to them. He told them to shower *before* work. He explained that they wouldn't be getting healthcare, as it's not a civil right, especially not for the irresponsibly rotund. He also didn't hit on them, which left them flabbergasted, and was the underlying primary motivator for their nonsensical PC language brigade.

Amy and Randi lawyered up and took B. Fingers to court for "toxic masculinity." The judge was a sensible person and told Amy and Randi to stop wasting his time. The next day, both women quit and became lifestyle bloggers, which were in *short supply*.

After such a close call, B. Fingers simply axed the childcare operation, and moved forward with things that actually mattered to his clients at the gym, like banana stations to keep potassium levels high.

Back at the staff party, B. Fingers announces that he's giving raises to everyone for outstanding work. Morale is at an all-time high because everyone is in shape, hot, and making money.

The End.

MICHAEL CZECH

"Mic check. Mic...check. 1, 2, 1, 2. Mic check," blasts over the stadium's P.A. system. "Yeah? What do you need?" responds the rookie concert audio engineer, Michael Czech. "No, not you, Mike Czech, I'm giving a mic check to check the mics!" exclaims his colleague, Fred Durst, who was no stranger to mic checks. Mike Czech fell for the "mic check," yet again.

Michael Czech had made an interesting lateral career choice. He left his former profession of cardiology for his true passion, wiring large-scale audio equipment for massive concerts. He knew his steady hands would benefit society more if he could help people enjoy getting trashed and taking drugs on a deeper level. Sure, he knew the performers and DJs got all the glory, but his line of logic was that just like cardiology, he could pull the plug and end the show.

Tonight's concert is already shaping up to be a fucking rager. Taylor Swift is the main event and Michael is horny as fuck, quite naturally though, as Mike Czech is a 48 year-old rhino with a massive horn that's fully torqued at all times.

Michael is on a tight deadline to finish the last part of the audio testing, the wireless mic setup, but can't help noticing Taylor Swift walk into her dressing room backstage. Michael fails to realize he's holding a hot mic that hadn't been properly checked. He absentmindedly pockets the unchecked mic, and stampedes backstage.

"Taylor, I just wanted to tell you first off that you shouldn't be alarmed that I'm blocking your escape," says Michael with the confidence of former Olympian Bruce Jenner. Taylor looks back at Michael with a disarming look in her eye and says, "You're lucky enough to be different, never change." Michael Czech looks confused. He entered the room with every intention of dropping his pants and furiously masturbating in front of Miss Swift. He skimmed the news occasionally and heard that was popular in entertainment these days. Meanwhile, the crowds of screaming teenagers and beta males pour into the stadium and hear the entire dialogue happening backstage.

"I'm here to set you up for a hard Mike Czech," Michael declares. Taylor responds, "My friends tease me about the fact that if someone seems bad or shady or like they have a secret, I find them incredibly interesting. Tell me more."

This was not the response Mike Czech was looking for, so he decided to lay it out plain and simple. "I was looking to expose myself to you in exchange for not ruining the audio quality of your show. Don't you get it?"

Taylor smiles and simply responds, "Yeah I get it. Why don't you just go and jackoff somewhere else?" Michael hadn't considered the notion that maybe some women don't respond favorably to fat, sexually frustrated men with zero sex appeal other than their position of professional leverage. Women with strong values and self-respect don't fall for sexual terrorism. "Well I'm not leaving until I blow a load on someone's chest," exclaims Dr. Czech.

Without saying a word, Taylor walks out of her dressing room to the stage. Mike Czech sits down and jacks off all over his own chest, all while crying and repeatedly shouting "FUCK THOTS!" His frustration was misguided, as he only had himself to blame for his failed sexual extortion.

Taylor's message and Michael's solo JO session echo throughout the stadium. Everyone in the stadium hears it. The girls start cheering, while the beta males in the stadium begin sobbing hysterically and drinking soymilk.

Michael is still teeming with rage, and rushes to the backstage audio booth, passes Taylor on his way and yells, "Looks like we're both in a sticky situation," and rips apart every wire he can. The stadium goes dark and the concert looks like it's over.

Then, out of nowhere, a helicopter rigged with really sweet speakers descends on the concert. It's none other than Brett Whiskers. He takes the stage with Taylor and they cover the song "Pimp Juice" by Nelly. In this moment, everything is right in the world.

The End.

DIEGO DONK

The shrill shriek of a whistle blows after a helmet-to-helmet collision. Yellow flags fly in the air, and a brawl breaks out between the two championship teams, the Vegas Gun Slingers and the Oklahoma City Who-Gives-a-Fucks. Dontavius Jackson and Dar'quellion Marshall are slow to get up as the rest of their teams engage in the exercise in futility that is punching each other in the facemasks.

The benches clear and calamity ensues. Guys like Kyle Turley and Bill Romanowski would be proud of the action.

The announcers in the press box desperately try to spin the action as a testament to the honest and appropriate response that multimillionaire professionals should have whenever their wildly violent sport has a marginally more violent outcome than the rules permit. "These guys really love each other and they always compete."

First on the scene is the Head Referee, Diego Donk. He's a middle-aged donkey with a track record of excellence. Donk graduated Magna Cum Laude from the Referee's Institute of Referees, and even gave the commencement speech. In said speech, he highlighted the primary responsibility of being a ref: to keep the players safe, let the players play, and keep the game fun.

To break up the fight, Donk shouts out, "I'll eject every last one of you so hard, you'll think Goose from Top Gun had it easy!" Everyone stops brawling out of respect, and the game resumes. The injured players are carted off the field giving the universal sign for "I'm potentially paralyzed from the waist down but I don't regret my career choice"...the hard thumbs up.

The announcers in the box mention that Diego Donk is a pro's pro, and that Ed Hochuli's officiating skills and biceps look fairly pedestrian by comparison.

The game rages on with a tight score of 20 to 27 in favor of the Gun Slingers. The Who-Gives-a-

Fucks drive down to the Vegas 3 yard line with 3 seconds left. The ball is snapped and the quarterback lasers a bullet to his favorite tight end, Aaron Hernandez. With the clock expired, the Oklahoma City team sets up for the game tying extra point.

Diego Donk secretly placed his entire life savings on a highly specific bet that the Who-Gives-a-Fucks would win in regulation. He got a hot tip from his wife's boyfriend, Banana Fingers. On the kick, Donk deliberately calls four false starts on the same lineman to push the extra point attempt far enough back that the coach of the OKC team decides to go for two.

Donk, the most respected ref in the history of refs, had just pulled a fast one. He had been pulling off underhanded stunts like this for years, but nobody batted an eye, because Donk literally wrote the book, "Who's Reffing the Ref? ETHICS IN REFFING".

It was genius, really. Donk could execute fixes and pulls all under the guise of being one of the good guys. Donk should've considered a career at the FBI with that sort of talent.

The odds appear astronomically stacked against the offense. The big Who-Gives-a-Fuck quarterback steps back as his receivers run streaks, then fucking launches a bomb to the end zone. The OKC receiver is well covered, but Diego Donk poetically and discreetly trips the Vegas defensive back, making it all appear accidental. With a Randy Moss-esque catch by the OKC receiver, the two-point conversion is good. Donk knows the rule that the ref is part of the field, and that with his track record of excellence, he wouldn't catch too much heat.

The 2009 Superbowl was in the books. After the game, Donk thought to himself that after this high profile hoodwink, he might have to lay low or possibly retire. He ultimately decided he would hide in plain sight by shifting to officiating women's basketball, which nobody watches anyway.

Diego took his winnings and bought a shit ton of bitcoins.

The End.

RICHARD KICKEM

"FUCK ME IN THE FUCKING DIRT-PIPE," yells the cocaine-fueled shell of a duck. Richard Kickem, the mallard with a taste for overconfidently making gargantuan bets, courting prostitutes, and drowning in spicy margaritas, just lost the biggest sports bet of his life.

Dick Kickem had been on a hot streak for years. His first major gambling victory came when he placed $20,000 on a prop bet with 500,000 to 1 odds. His bet was that Dale Earnhardt Senior would die in the final lap of the 1998 Daytona 500. He won 10 billion dollars.

He immediately went from being a former underpaid I.T.T. Tech "C" student to an international playboy. He started gambling on anything and everything, all while chasing the nearly cardiac arrest-inducing rush of his prodigiously improbable NASCAR bet.

He started placing bets on everything he could, and somehow continued to win big. It was as if he had advanced knowledge of everything on which he bet. From putting his entire fortune on Kelly Clarkson winning the first season of American Idol, to the Red Sox winning the 2004 World Series, Dick Kickem couldn't lose. It was entirely unclear why he was allowed in Vegas after nearly ruining the city's economy over a 5-year period.

On his rise to becoming a trillionaire, Dick started to develop a taste for the finer things in life: namely cocaine, tequila, and morally destitute women he found on social media. He quickly lost interest in anything that wasn't outrageously expensive and/or degrading to other people. He was on a search for meaning.

He bought a fleet of Ferraris with a matching fleet of midgets and made them perform demolition derbies. He bought a space shuttle and launched it into the cosmos, full of all the research known to man about curing cancer. He tried jumping a steamroller, Evil Kinevil style, over 50 senior citizens laid side by side. He exclusively ate endangered species. It all sounded so good on paper, but none of it brought him the joy he expected.

Dick Kickem's winning streak finally came to an abrupt end in 2009 on a single bet, the Superbowl. How did Dick Kickem end up in this mess in the first place? For starters, misstep number one was graduating from I.T.T. Tech. He worked as a network specialist at Brett Whisker's building and broke into B-Dubs apartment. There, in all its glory, was Brett Whiskers' secret time machine. Dick decided that navigating the space-time continuum would be a breeze, and took himself back in time. It worked out so well for Michael J. Fox, why not him?

Unfortunately, after all those years of gambling wizardry, he had finally caught up to the timeline through which he had transported. He lost all his advanced knowledge of world events and summarily lost his de facto superpower of foresight.

This was the end of the line for Dick Kickem. He placed his multi trillion-dollar fortune on the Vegas Gun Slingers and lost it all. A decade of decadence, mountains of blow, enough spicy margaritas to fill a Sea World orca tank, and about three tons of high-priced syphilitic vagina were gone in an instant.

"That fucking ref just fucked me," Dick shouts at the top of his lungs. A huge gorilla sits across the bar from Dick. "When you don't ref yourself, a ref might start reffing your lack of reffing and ref you into an un-reffable situation." This was indeed the gorilla, Banana Fingers, who was on his yearly vacation in Vegas.

"I bet it's not the last time you'll get fucked, either, " exclaims B. Fingers. "You're right. I'll take that bet." Then in front of the entire Vegas ESPN Zone, Dick Kickem drops his pants and walks backward towards the gorilla. He's at the lowest point in his life. The gorilla turns Dick back around and punches him in the face. "You really misread what I was saying."

The End.

JERRY JERRYSON

Jerry had terrible luck with women, and felt like online dating was his only chance at finding a normal female. He had been on two dates from his favorite dating app and both women seemed to be anxiously depressed messes, but he figured he was just unlucky. These women were probably exceptions to the high quality, marriage-worthy gals he anticipated were in extreme abundance.

There were so many beautiful women on the apps, even if only about 1 in 12 were 8s and 9s. Jerry knew if he just put the right pictures and bio on his profile, he'd find a woman worth her weight in gold. Ironically, on a literal level, if some of these women were, he'd be a billionaire.

Jerry elected to portray himself as a dog-loving family man who was always at the beach, despite the fact that he spent most of his time playing Fortnite, jacking off incessantly, and watching Pewdiepie videos. Jerry saw himself as an alpha, but was just a potbelly pig in extreme denial. He was overweight, didn't have a career going, his eyes were too close together, and his chin was nearly concave. He also had a micropenis.

"It's a match!" read the explosively cartoonish notification on the smartphone. After about five thousand swipes, Jerry had finally matched with a girl. Her profile description made her seem pretty solid: "If you can't handle me at my worst, you don't deserve me at my best" was the first line of her "about me" section. The description continued with: "I have two kids, I'm not looking for hookups, I want a gentleman who is over six feet tall, has a lot of money, isn't bald or balding, and who wants to travel all the time. You must love to laugh, love eating good food, and love animals."

"Wow this girl is unique. Who would think in this day and age that someone would have such niche viewpoints?" thought Jerry. "Plus, her photos where she doesn't show her body and covers her face with massive sunglasses makes her pretty mysterious—which is hot."

Jerry met up with his match at the fanciest steakhouse in town, Roasties. She must have

weighed about a deuce, possibly a deuce and a half. Jerry immediately regretted the meet-up, but he was stuck there, and didn't have the courage to tell her she was a 5/10 on an academic scale. She got drunk as a skunk within the first 15 minutes, so Jerry knew she possessed the perfect mix of confidence and self-esteem. Maybe her disregard for taking care of herself physically was her only shortcoming, Jerry thought to himself.

"So tell me about yourself," inquired Jerry. "Well, I've never been on one of these dates before. I can't believe I'm actually on a dating app," responded the sweaty hog across the table. This was an outright lie, but admitting to sexual tourism on dating apps was a faux pas, and most of the users were happy to take a stance of willful ignorance to the fact that modern dating was more of a sexual carousel than a romantic fairytale.

"Wow, I really appreciate your honesty," responded Jerry, who played along with the charade.

"Yeah, my friends tell me I'm too real sometimes," fired back Jerry's date. She was edgy.

Back at Jerry's apartment, the two started making out and quickly got naked. Jerry held back the urge to ralph. "I never do this," exclaimed Jerry's date. Jerry tried to interpret this as a sign that he had tons of game, and that no woman could resist his charm. Jerry's cognitive dissonance was nearly pathological.

After a short lived sexual encounter, Jerry and his date felt disgusted, both with each other and themselves. What had just transpired was cheap and inauthentic at best. Some might have even described it as transactional. As they got dressed, they both doubled down on their nearly shattered fragile egos and narcissistically thought to themselves, "I can do better than this, I deserve to date a 10."

Jerry got herpes, by the way.

The End.

GEORGE MONOCLE

The retiree strolls through the Darbyshire University Library, tapping his fingers on the book-ends as he passes them. Pacing down the aisles in the labyrinth of knowledge feels familiar to George Monocle, the introverted and scholarly badger who typifies the archetypal, industry-standard, proud badger with a strong lineage who enjoys reading, playing chess, smoking cigars, and an occasional snuff film.

The elderly male librarian passes by and tells George, "It's a fine day for learning something new!"

George barely audibly mumbles back, "A fine day for you to shut the fuck up in the library. Christ."

"What was that?" The librarian clarifies. "Oh, I said, do you have anything in here that I haven't read before?" Although the Darbyshire University Library was massive, George Monocle had read nearly every book in its halls.

Before the librarian could respond, a small earthquake rattles the library, and two books fall off the shelf adjacent to George, hitting him in the head. He picks one up, and reads the title out loud. "'Fully Torqued: Why Kegels Are for Everyone,' by Banana Fingers." George casts the book aside to pick up the second volume. It's titled "The Internet". George turns to the librarian and asks "Excuse me, but what is 'The Internet'?"

The librarian tells George it's a place for sharing ideas, and contains a compendium of basically every book ever written. He also explains that it's chock-full of porn.

"What's porn?" George inquires. "It's what's ruining sexual relations, male creativity, and overall motivation in the world. It's also pretty hot," mentions the librarian.

"Oh yeah, you can also buy weed online, too," remarks the bibliothecary. "What's weed?" asks George. "Well, you smoke it, and it makes music better, movies funnier, and makes pseudo-intellectuals tell stories that never go anywhere, all while assuming a position of moral superiority. You can read all about it on social media," declares the bibliosoph.

"Social media?" asks George. "Yeah, it's essentially a series of heavily-censored websites where people share pictures with meaningless captions, express opinions on subjects of which they have zero knowledge, and validate their own thoughts in proverbial echo chambers that perpetuate their own ignorance," announces the librarian. "Oh ok, I think I get it," enthusiastically professes George.

George Monocle buys a computer on his way home. He reads the instruction manual, and logs into his neighbor's Wi-Fi. After creating a gaggle of internet accounts, he creates an Instagram profile and posts an image of a wooden spoon with the caption: "dance like nobody's watching." It gets 1 like and George feels devastated.

He follows up with a trip to anal911.com, but can't find any straightforward quality badger videos, so he settles for the most-viewed/"hottest" page full of incestuous anal videos — lots of teenage foxes getting destroyed physically, mentally, emotionally, and spiritually. George throws up in his mouth and moves on.

He then orders some weed for delivery. When it arrives, he smokes it, then immediately posts to Facebook: "Life is offensive." Most of the responses contain at least one of the words: racist, sexist, homophobic, bigot, privilege, or "I'm with Her." George sobers up, realizing that sharing his thoughts with strangers is as useless as their responses.

At this point, George concludes that the Internet sounds much better on paper than in reality. George returns to the library the next day. "Give me the book about kegels, please."

The End.

JOHNNY THUNDER

"And that's how you take a 1031 exchange all the way to the bank. Remember, time is money and knowledge is power. If money makes you powerful, then time is knowledge. Thank you," concluded Johnny Thunder, the kangaroo boxer turned motivational speaker. The crowd of primarily middle-aged divorced realtors erupted with cheers, applause, and unbridled enthusiasm. "Wow, I'm so jacked up right now, I could buy a Tony Robbins motivational audiobook," exclaimed a fat man wearing a Hawaiian shirt. "I made the right choice not having a family so I could pursue my childhood passion of renovating foreclosed rental properties," chimed in a depressed-looking woman whose appearance screamed: "my house smells like cat shit—deal with it."

This was the effect Johnny Thunder always had on his crowds. He wasn't always this kind of kangaroo, though. In fact, his entire public persona was a facade. When he was twenty, he narrowly avoided a stint of jail time for beating the living shit out of his effeminate neighbor. Johnny assumed his neighbor wanted to blow him, when in actuality, his neighbor was just a run-of-the-mill Canadian.

Johnny was a rough kid from a damaged family and fighting was his primary outlet, but the threat of living out the rest of his days in a maximum security prison as the resident BJ technician didn't rank too highly on his list of life aspirations.

His life changed one day when he watched the movie "Limitless". NZT was clearly and unmistakably a pseudonym and near advertisement for ADHD stimulant medications. Johnny went to his local psychiatrist and requested an Adderall prescription. Per industry standard, the doctor wrote the prescription without asking any questions. He also wrote Johnny a Xanax prescription for good measure.

Johnny wasn't a big reader, and played by his own rules, so he took three times the amount of his pills as was prescribed. In a drug-fueled stupor, Johnny felt compelled to clean his entire house. He then realized he could do this on a much larger scale, so Johnny started flipping foreclosed properties. The Darbyshire Gazette took notice of the "high-energy" kangaroo who was turning the shittiest properties in the city into marginally less shitty properties. Johnny was on fire.

Johnny was asked to speak at a local Ted Talk and took the stage, high as a kite. He opened up by telling the crowd that life was about playing to win, and that taking no for an answer was a surefire way to lose big. The blasé rapists in the crowd rolled their eyes because they already knew this, but the rest of the crowd reveled in the empty catchphrases and recycled rallying cries of literally every motivational speaker on the planet. The crowds loved him so much that he soon began his own podcast/webinar series, and wrote a book: "Thunder is Lighting: Flip the Flop".

Johnny rode the meth train all the way to big time and there was no end in sight. Johnny was scheduled for his annual motivational seminar, ThunderCon, and knew that he had to be absolutely on-point. He stepped up like a pro and smoked a bag of meth before hitting the stage.

"Thunder and Lightning is about breaking through barriers, breaking through boundaries, and breaking the rules. Any questions before I begin?" asked Johnny. "Did you vote for Hillary?" blurted out an archetypal neck-bearded blogger sitting in the front row.

Johnny was so trashed that he broke character. He lost the ability to continue being a method actor right on the spot. Johnny jumped off stage and began beating the blogger senseless. It was as if the blogger were Canadian, and they were the only two people in the auditorium.

When Johnny finally got ahold of himself, he looked around as a sea of filming camera phones surrounded him. He stood up, collected himself, and exclaimed, "Lesson 1: Ask better questions."

The crowd of mindless simpletons vomited cheers of exaltation. Amidst the din, a father turned to his son and shouted, "Not all heroes wear capes, son!"

The End.

DAMIEN SMITE

"COME OUT AND FACE ME, YOU COWARDLY POTBELLY PIG DEMON! I WILL OBLITERATE YOUR COURAGE AND CAST YOU BACK TO THE NEVER-ENDING WATERFALL OF GARBAGE YOU CAME FROM!" Damien Smite yelled at his passed out roommate, Garth. Damien was an exorcist in training, and took every opportunity possible to bloviate power phrases he intended on using one day when the time came for him to cast a creature of hell back from whence it came. Friday nights after hitting the club were no exception.

Garth woke up confused, and still slightly shitfaced. "What the fucking fuck is going on?" he inquired.

"I feared your soul had been harvested by a nameless malice from the inner caverns of Hades, my friend," calmly replied Damien.

"Dude, it's really weird when you say shit like that. Can't we ever have a chill night out, and possibly play it cool enough to bring some girls back to the apartment?" pleaded Garth.

Damien walked outside to the balcony and drew in a deep breath of the crisp winter air. "The only kind of chill night I want is the frost-laden absence of Lucifer's hellhounds expelled back into oblivion."

Damien was a complicated raven. On one hand, he had a surprisingly robust vocabulary, and a strangely poetic way of describing the world. On the other hand, he chose to use his linguistic skills on a faux-profession that was made popular by a movie in 1973.

The next night, Damien and Garth went out to the newly opened club called Night Shade. Damien wore his signature outfit: a trench coat, John Lennon bifocals, and a necklace with a flask of holy water attached. Garth dressed like a normal person. After waiting in line for over an hour, the two friends entered the club.

After a few drinks, Damien began inspecting women who he thought might have been possessed. He invaded their personal space and invoked the courage of the Lord to give him the power to see through the trickery of Hell. Garth couldn't believe that Damien was fouling up another night out.

"Dude, you've gotta lock this shit up. I haven't gotten laid in months because you keep chasing off every girl in sight, especially the tipsy ones, who are my best shot," complained Garth. Garth's physical appearance was markedly off-putting, so drunk women were his only option.

It then dawned on Damien. These women weren't possessed, but were being over-served by the Demon of Gluttony, Beelzebub. Damien flew over to the barkeep and slapped him furiously with his wings. Garth looked over at the action briefly, and then turned back to the gal in front of him who gleefully exclaimed, "I hate fights, let's get out of here." Damien had inadvertently and somehow literally pulled through as a wingman.

"I SUMMON THE STRENGTH OF *HE WHO IS CALLED I AM* TO THWART YOUR DEMONIACAL CAMPAIGN OF CARNAGE WAGED VENGEFULLY ON THE FAIR DAMES OF HUMANITY!" called out Damien.

This was the bartender's first night working, and he didn't know what to do. He also happened to have Aspberger's, which made reading the situation far more difficult.

"So do you want a beer or a cocktail?" offered the bartender.

"I INVOKE THE FATHER, SON, AND HOLY SPIRIT TO BANISH YOU BACK TO THE SULFURIC PLANE OF THE MELANCHOLIC INFERNO!" blasted back Damien.

The bartender responded, "I don't think we have that. Here's a bud light."

Damien saw right through this act, and smashed the beer bottle and his holy water on the bartender's head, knocking him unconscious.

"*Requiesca en pace*, Beelzebub. Your days of glutinous terror are no more."

Damien casually walked outside the bar, fired up a cigarette, and was then promptly arrested for assault.

The End.

MILTON THE BRAVE

"Look both ways before you cross, guys!" yelled the volunteer school crossing guard to the small group of elementary school students. Milton valued the safety of children above anything else in life.

"Back the fuck up, lady! You're encroaching on my crosswalk! I will blow up your car with a pipe bomb!!" belted Milton as he blew his Hello Kitty plastic whistle at an SUV that was idling a healthy twelve feet back from him. Milton, the otherwise unemployed ostrich, took his job far too seriously.

The school principal was constantly second-guessing whether or not she should fire someone who worked for free. Milton was a liability, but also a damn good crossing guard. His enthusiasm, hustle, and lateral footwork made him the Ron Artest of volunteering.

It was 3:30, and there was just one group of students left to cross the street. As the children began to walk across on Milton's signal, an unfamiliar, unmarked van pulled up. The woman inside told the kids to get in. They all piled in mid-cross, as Milton watched in horror. Milton ran in front of the car, and pulled out his pepper spray. He approached the driver side window and unleashed a full canister of police-grade Mace in the driver's face. He then pulled her out of the car, and proceeded to kick her in the face—repeatedly. The children started cheering, because they had been properly conditioned to equate violence with entertainment.

"You think you can abduct children on my crosswalk? Who sent you? Who do you work for?" interrogated Milton. "I'm the housekeeper," the woman whimpered.

"The Housekeeper, eh? That must be your *gang name*! Go back to your boss and tell him I'm coming for him next." Milton turned to the kids and yelled, "The show's not over yet, guys. Run for your lives!" Then he slashed the van's tires and set it on fire to punctuate his personal belief that organized crime required vigilante justice.

The next day Milton woke up to a phone call. "Hey, so you assaulted my housekeeper and blew up my van. You're in deep shit, bucko."

"So you're the one running the child trafficking operation, then? Your days are numbered," Milton fired back. Milton clearly didn't have a firm grasp on how modern child trafficking rings operated these days, but his intentions were pure. Milton knew over 800,000 kids went missing each year, and wasn't about to allow this to happen to on his watch.

"What the fuck are you talking about?" asked the unknown caller.

Milton hung up the phone, dialed *69, cross-referenced whitepages.com, and drove over to the location of the boss. He rang the doorbell with the bellicosity of a meth head on a steroid binge. An oversized grizzly bear opened the door. "Hi, can I help you?" asked Tench Trenchpipe, the homeowner standing opposite Milton.

"I'm here for combat," announced Milton, as his adrenal glands pushed him closer and closer to an aggravated assault charge.

"I like your intensity. You strike me as the kind of guy who takes a driver to a par three course, and I respect that. Reminds me a bit of myself back when I was in the army. In fact, we could use some new recruits. It's a volunteer position, but it's worth it," explained Tench.

"I fucking love volunteering," replied Milton.

The End.

Closing Remarks

Wow, that was a lot to unpack.

To the people who enjoyed at least part the book, thank you!

To those who might be feeling uncomfortable, angry, perplexed, hateful, resentful, or otherwise, ask yourself why. If this collection of fictitious short stories triggers intolerable discomfort, so much that you project an annihilation fantasy on the author and the readers who enjoyed the book, realize that your reaction is your own, and it speaks volumes about you. If you think "hate speech" is the problem with the stories, you might just be brainwashed...

As my great friend once wrote to me:

"We have evolved to survive, but not evolved to be happy. Most people have convinced themselves of the opposite, and that they and everyone else deserve both, based on nothing other than subscribing to a utopian fantasy. Social cohesion cannot exist in narrow and fragmented reality, where everyone pilots his or her own ship based on emotion alone. Anchoring in truth rather than in ever-expanding ideals is key. We can best understand truth through logic, evidence, tradition, family, self-examination, courage, and a splash of humor to make the unhappy discomfort of the world tolerable. A word of advice about subjective and relativistic reality: you can choose to live in avoidance of reality, but you cannot avoid the consequences of doing so. We live in a time of outrage culture, identity politics, perpetual victimhood, censorship, and emotionally driven, ideological mob lynching on the Internet. It's time we choose what our anchoring points are and stick to them. Techno-progressivism has a stranglehold on many wonderful people, and weak men stand by and allow it. Stand up or live in shame and cowardice. Right?"

-P.S.

Get ready for the second book, because Darbyshire isn't finished yet.

CPSIA information can be obtained
at www.ICGtesting.com
Printed in the USA
LVHW071143050119
602508LV00001B/1/P